Bella's Den

For the Hardy Family

CONTENTS

Chapter 1
A secret

We always came down the lane on our horses.

We galloped faster and faster and mud flew all round us. Polly the sheepdog jumped along behind. We had to rein the horses in really hard when we got to the farm gate in case they tried to leap over and sent us flying.

Then we tied them to the fence. Bella's horse was called Lightning and mine was called Splash. We left them at the fence because they'd never make it past the next bit.

They weren't really horses, you see. They were bikes.

Bella and I had been playing horses for weeks when she told me about her den. She had never told anyone else about it, and she had to get to know me pretty well before she told me.

I had millions of friends where I lived before, all in my street, and all the way down town to school. But in my new house, there was only one person to play with for miles, and that was Bella. There was Polly too, but she didn't count because she was a dog and she couldn't come out with us at lambing time.

So it was a good job I got on with Bella.

But I didn't always.

The thing was that Bella had an annoying habit of vanishing.

Sometimes, if we had an argument about whose horse had won or whose turn it was to close the farm gate, she would just stand there. Her face closed up as if she was thinking, 'I don't have to play with you, you know.' I'd go back to shut the gate and she'd vanish. I didn't know how she did it. Polly vanished too.

Bella had a secret, and she was pretty good at keeping it.

It was no use waiting for them or shouting their names. I'd just have to wheel my bike back home and sit watching telly. I watched telly a lot when we first came to our new house.

Then one day Bella seemed to decide that I really was her friend.

It was her turn to shut the farm gate and I said, "Bella, I wish you'd tell me where you go when you vanish."

And she did.

Chapter 2
Nobody but me

This is what you do.

You stand by the fence just where there's a muddy patch. It's where the barbed wire has been stretched. You look both ways, up and down the lane. Then you duck under the wire and slither down a really steep slope. It's no good if you cling on to plants or branches because they come away in your hands. But if you look down you can just make out Bella's path. It's a thin zigzag line, like the tracks that sheep and rabbits make.

You have to roll down the last bit – there's
no other way. And then you have to jump up

sharp because you've come to the river. It isn't very wide just there, so it's easy to leap across it. You'd better have wellies on in case you don't make it.

Now you're on a little hill with no grass on the top. There are holes in it. Scramble up this hill and duck under some branches. And then you're there!

"There," Bella says. "My den."

The roots of a tree jut out like a shelf, and under them it is hollow. Strands of grass and moss hang over it. When you lift them up, there's a bit of an old ladder and part of a crate to make a door. There's a sheep's skull nailed onto the door. Some of its teeth are missing and it has half a horn broken off.

You crawl in through the door and pull the grasses down. It's dark and damp and it smells of earth. It smells a million years old.

Bella's Den

BERLIE DOHERTY

With illustrations by
Ellie Snowdon

Barrington Stoke

Published in 2018 in Great Britain by
Barrington Stoke Ltd
18 Walker Street, Edinburgh, EH3 7LP

www.barringtonstoke.co.uk

Text © 1997, 2018 Berlie Doherty
Illustrations © 2018 Ellie Snowdon

A CIP catalogue record for this book is available
from the British Library upon request

ISBN: 978-1-78112-811-4

Printed in China by Leo

And there you are – where nobody can see you. But you can see out. It's so still. All you can hear is the river, like a long, long sigh.

"I bet nobody ever comes here," I whisper.

"Nobody knows about it," Bella whispers back, "but me."

And me now.

But that's not all.

Chapter 3
Treasure

If you scramble out of the den and look round
in the bed of mosses by the hill, you can see
there's a loose tufty bit. Lift it up and you've
found the treasure trove. There are bits
of old cups and plates with lovely patterns.
Some of them have gold on too. And there's a
Father Christmas badge with a bent pin.

That's still not all. There are pools around
here that nobody would find even if they came
looking for them.

There's Midge Pool and the Bog of Eternal
Stench, Rowan Hole and Stink Weed Bog
(that's where we empty out our cups of nettle
tea). Over there in the leaf bed is where the

hedgehogs sleep. They'll be there till spring. And there's Mini-Beast House, where we put all the insects and bugs that need looking after.

And that's still not all. Below the hill with no grass, there's a patch of earth that's all black, dark soil. At one time nothing grew there at all. But do you see those trees? You might think they are just twigs, but they're growing, they really are.

"They're two times as big as they were when we put them in last year," Bella tells me.

"We?"

"Tom and Jessica."

When Bella talks about Tom and Jessica, I feel really upset. This is *our* den. It belongs to me and Bella. I've never even heard of Tom and Jessica.

"You said you hadn't told anyone else about it," I say. I feel like pulling up those twigs.

"I found it at the same time as they did. We were together," Bella says. "So how could I have told them about it? We planted the trees the day they left, ages before you came. One tree each."

"Don't they come any more?" I say. I am starting to feel a bit better.

"Of course they don't," Bella tells me. "You've moved into their house. They live miles and miles away now. Nobody comes here, I told you. Nobody but me. I come every now and again to tidy up. I'm looking after it. But it's not as good, on my own."

Chapter 4
Moons on the grass

It was a long time before I went back to the den.

Bella didn't ask me, and I didn't think I should go there without her. I told myself it was a silly sort of den anyway. I missed my friends. In my old house, we didn't need dens.

But then one day, Bella showed me its real secret, its deep-down dark secret. After that, I knew for sure that it was the most special place in the world, and that it was just as much mine as Bella's.

It was a kind of dare at first.

Bella was staying at my house for the night because her mum and dad were going to be out late. My mum let us sleep out in the garden in Bella's tent. There is a little campsite out in the field at the back of the cottages, but that belongs to the farm. I like to watch the campers sometimes. At night, their tents glow like coloured moons on the grass. Bella and I didn't have a torch or a lamp in our tent. You don't need one when the moon is as full as it was that night.

We couldn't sleep because the tawny owls were having a chat, one in each tree in the garden. They sounded like people with really bad colds sneezing their heads off. First one would sneeze and make you jump out of your skin. And then you'd be just about to drift off to sleep when another one would answer.

The tawny owls kept this up for over an hour. I wanted to climb up the trees and shoo them away.

Bella squirmed out of her sleeping bag and started to pull on her wellies.

"Where are you going?" I asked.

"The den, of course."

"Now?"

She was off before I had a chance to ask any more questions. She vanished again. It took me five seconds to know what I had to do. If Bella could vanish, then so could I.

I put my sleeping bag round me like a cloak, stuck my bare feet in my wellies and grabbed the packet of sweets.

By this time Bella was out of sight.

Our bikes were in the shed and it would
have made too much noise to get them out. So

I flopped across the farmyard after Bella till
I'd got my feet into my wellies, then I ran over
the bridge and up the lane and looked in the
moonlight for the muddy patch. My sleeping
bag ripped a bit on the barbed wire and I knew
I had to come back the next day to look for
any torn bits on the fence. It was important

that we never left any clues that would show someone else the way.

Then I slipped and slid all the way down the bank. I didn't yell out. My sleeping bag fell off when I was crossing the river, and I stung myself on some nettles.

But it was all worth it. Every little bit of agony was worth it, because of what happened next.

Chapter 5
The middle of the world

We must have been in the den for almost an hour. There wasn't room for us both to lie down, so we sat crouched together with Bella's sleeping bag pulled across us both.

We were both staring out into the night. It was so dark that it was like a black curtain, just too far away to reach out and touch.

Then the moon slid away from the clouds and shone over the grass that covered the den.

All of a sudden it was as bright as day. And I think I was the first to see it.

I was looking at the big mound below the den. I was thinking how the moon made it look like a stage with the lights on, and how deep and black those holes were, when I saw something move.

I touched Bella's arm and she let out a little breath of, *yes, I've seen it too*.

It was a fox.

He grew out of the darkness of the hole, and then took shape as the moon lit him. He stood as if he had been turned to stone, and he was looking right at our den, right past the grassy strands, right at me.

It was as if he was locked into me, reading my mind. I didn't dare move or breathe. I didn't dare do anything but look back at him, till my eyes blurred.

I was holding myself so still that I thought
I would pass out. My skin was ice-cold, frozen
cold with fear.

Then all of a sudden the fox seemed to relax. He turned his head just a little, and, as if it was a signal, out came another fox and three little cubs. Four shapes loomed out of the hole, each one faster than the one before. They were jumping out like little kids in a school playground, tumbling red and brown and silvery white.

The dog fox slunk off into the shadows.

The other big fox, his vixen, sat just where he had been, at the front of the hole. She pricked up her ears and her head turned from time to time as she listened out for all kinds of sounds in the hills.

But the three cubs had come out to play. They biffed each other and fell over and rolled about. They jumped on each other, jumped on the vixen, hid from each other and played roly-poly right down to the river.

I could hear them breathing, and scuffling with their paws. I could hear the little puffs of sound they made when they biffed each other.

It felt as if this little patch of ground where the foxes were playing was the middle of the world. It felt as if nothing else that was happening anywhere was as important as this.

I've no idea what the signal was but, quick as a flash, the vixen turned her head, sharp. The cubs scrambled up the bank and one by one slid back into the hole. The vixen waited a moment, lifted her head then melted down into the hole after them. She slid into it like water.

It went dark again, as if the moon had been put out.

I'm not sure if I really saw it or not, but then I think I saw another shape, like a dark flutter where the hole was, and a dull white glow like the tip of a tail vanishing into it.

Chapter 6
Never, never, never

Next day I was so excited. I wanted to tell someone about the fox.

"I've seen a fox," I said to my mum. "A real fox. And all its cubs. Three of them! They were playing!"

We were standing in the farmyard as I told her this. Bella had just come running towards me from her cottage, and the farmer came out of the lambing shed at the same time. He stood and looked down at me.

"Where did you see this fox?" he asked me.

I waved my arm over to where Bella's den was, and then I saw the look on Bella's face. I couldn't believe what I'd done.

"Where exactly?" the farmer asked.

I shook my head. "I d-don't remember," I stammered.

Mum looked at me oddly.

"Vixen and three cubs?" the farmer asked me again.

I nodded. I couldn't look him in the eyes any more. I couldn't look at my mum. Bella had turned her back on me. I felt sick.

"You know what foxes do, don't you?" the farmer said. "They bite the heads off the baby lambs!"

Bella started to run back to her cottage. I ran after her. She shut her gate so I couldn't follow her in.

"You're not to go to my den again," she said. Her voice was like ice. "Never, never, never."

I went back to my house and up to my room. All the joy of last night had vanished.

I wished I could un-say what I'd said. I wished I could say, "It wasn't true. I didn't really see a fox," or "It wasn't over there. It was the other way, over past the railway track."

But it was too late.

From my window I saw the sheep grazing, fields and fields of them. They had lambs by their sides. Lots of the lambs were new-borns, with little bendy legs and waggy tails. The older ones were already learning to play with each other. They were bounding up the little haystacks the farmer made for them, taking it in turns to jump off and run back up the stack.

I remembered what we'd seen. I remembered the dog fox, the secret fox, slinking off into the moonlit fields. What would he feed his cubs on, when they tumbled back down into their own den?

Now I would never see them again.

Chapter 7
The fun of it

That night I saw the farmer going down the lane with his gun. I ran back into our house and sobbed and sobbed.

Mum held me in her arms and said, "It's the farmer's business, not ours. He has to look after his sheep. It's his job."

But nothing would comfort me.

I didn't know what to say to Bella. It was the end of being friends. There was no more paddling in the river in our wellies, no more riding down the lane on Splash and Lightning. I knew I would never dare go to our den again.

We got on the school bus every day and sat at different ends of it, just the two of us.

"I wish I didn't live here!" I said to Mum. "I hate it! I wish we could move."

"What is it?" Mum asked, worried. "What is it you don't like about living here?"

I couldn't tell her. It was everything. I'd lost Bella, I'd lost the den, and I'd lost the fox.

*

One day I was brave enough to ask the farmer about it.

His name was Robert and he was always making jokes and laughing with us. I had to know if he really would shoot the foxes, even if Mum said it was none of my business.

I went up to Robert as he cleaned out the
sheep pens one day. I made a fuss of Meg, the
dog, and then I said, "Robert, do you really
shoot foxes?"

He stood up and looked at me as if I was a bit daft.

Then he said, "I don't kill foxes for the fun of it, you know. But if they bother my sheep, I do. Yes."

I didn't know what that meant. I didn't know if Robert's answer made me feel better or not.

Chapter 8
Skylark

It's funny, but in the end, it wasn't us who moved. It was Bella and her family. Her father had got a new job, in the Lake District.

"It'll be wonderful for them," Mum said. "Even more lovely than here. But poor Bella! She doesn't want to move one bit. Her mother can't get a smile out of her these days."

The next day I saw Bella on the school bus, and I wished I could say something to her. But

she just sat with her head down and wouldn't
look back at me.

On the day that Bella's family were moving house, Mum went down to give Bella's mum and dad a hand. "Come and say goodbye to her," she said to me. "You used to be such good friends!"

But there was no one in when we knocked at the door. Bella's mother and Polly came running down the lane towards us.

"I can't find Bella!" Bella's mum gasped. "I've looked everywhere!"

"I'll help," Mum said. "Have you tried all the barns?"

They ran off together, with Polly jumping along after them. But I didn't follow them. I knew exactly where Bella was.

I ran down the lane, past the gate, and up to the fence by the muddy patch. I looked both ways, up and down the lane. Then I ducked under the wire and slithered down the slope, as close to the thin zigzag track as I could. I rolled down the last bit, and jumped up sharp when I came to the river. I jumped across it.

Now I was on the little hill with no grass and the holes at the bottom. I scrambled up and ducked under the branches and there it was.

Bella's den.

"Bella?" I shouted.

I could hear her sniffing.

I sat just outside the den. I didn't know what to say to her. But I didn't want to leave her. It was really hot. There were swallows darting just above the river, catching insects. Miles above me I could hear the song of a skylark. It was too tiny to see.

"I'm sorry you're going, Bella," I said.

She sniffed.

"I'd hate to have to move," I said.

Another sniff.

"And I'm ... I'm sorry about the foxes."

There, I'd said it at last. After all those weeks.

"The foxes?"

Just as she said that, the air seemed to go silent. I felt something ripple down the back of my neck, as if the hairs were standing on end. Have you ever had the feeling that you were being watched?

I turned my head, very slowly, and there it was looking at me, looking right into me, right into my head. It was the fox. We stared at each other. Then it sank down away from sight and into its den.

I was so excited that I could hardly breathe. I wanted to scream with laughter. I wanted to roll about on the slope that the cubs had played on all those weeks ago. I wanted to tumble down it and splash into the river and scramble up again. I wanted to sing louder than the skylark.

I pulled Bella out of her den and danced about with her. At first she tried to pull away from me and then she started to laugh. We were both yelling with laughter. We swung each other round and round until we couldn't stay on our feet any longer.

"You're my best friend, Bella!" I shouted.

"You're mine!" she shouted back.

"I won't forget you!" I yelled.

"Never, never, never!" she hollered back.

Chapter 9
A secret shared

I often go to the den now. I tidy round a bit
and look after the trees that are growing here.
I look after Bella's twig – the one we planted
together.

When I've tidied round I always go and
crawl into the den. I huddle right in so nobody
can see me, but I can see out. It's so still. All
you can hear is the river, like a long, long sigh.

That's when the fox comes out. He always stares at me the same way, looking right in my eyes, right inside my head.

We share each other's secret.

It's so quiet here, you see. There's nothing to scare him away.

I haven't told anyone else about the den. I'm only telling you now because one day, if something happens to stop me from coming here, it will need looking after.

It's Bella's den, you see. And it's very special.

Our books are tested
for children and young people by
children and young people.

Thanks to everyone who consulted on
a manuscript for their time and effort in
helping us to make our books better
for our readers.